I0759884

FREAKS OF LIGHTNING

Art and Stories

Ryan George Kittleman

ISBN: 978-0-9849575-6-9

Published by:
Half A Library
P.O. Box 5115
Richmond, California
94805

Previous Publications:
"Thirst Trap" was originally published in *The North American Review*; "Never Forget a Face" in *The Charleston Anvil*; "Ribbon Cutting" in *Bat City Review*; "I Saw You Standing There" in *Mayday Magazine*; "Unlodging" in *Willows Wept*; and "The Bad Boy of Beef Lake" in *The Genre Society*.

Adaptations:
"Bad Boy of Beef Lake" was adapted into the film *Beefy!*; and "How to Hold a Garage Sale" was adapted into a film of the same name.

FREAKS OF LIGHTNING

Table of Contents

Stories

Art

The Living Curio

•••

Every morning, Alderman Boyle performed the same routine at the water pump. He hung his wig on the handle, bent his head beneath the spout, and worked the lever with one hand while scrubbing his scalp with the other. The wig sat on the handle like a small, patient animal waiting to be reunited with its owner.

On a Tuesday in October, Boyle was sluicing his noggin and pondering the flow of city drainage when a boy appeared at his elbow. The boy was out of breath. Boyle was not. Boyle had rarely, in his professional life, been out of breath.

"Sir," the boy said. "Mr. Dowe sent me. He needs a gentleman of distinction immediately."

"For what purpose?"

"He didn't say."

"And of all the gentlemen in town, you chose me?"

"You were the nearest."

Boyle considered this. It wasn't flattering, but it was accurate. He returned the wig to his head, adjusted it for symmetry, and followed the boy into town.

Mr. Dowe ran a coffeehouse called The Living Curio. Boyle had passed it many times without entering. He understood it to be the sort of establishment where clerks and students sat for long periods without buying very much. He had no particular opinion of the place and didn't expect to form one today.

The boy led him through the front room, which was empty, and into a back parlor that was not. The parlor was lined with display cases. Inside the cases were objects. Boyle noted, in order of appearance: the articulated skeleton of a guinea pig; a frog suspended in a jar of yellow liquid; a tobacco pipe said to have belonged to the King of Morocco; a pair of nun's stockings whose provenance was unknown; a lock of hair labeled *Cromwell, probably*; and a single dried pea identified only as *The Pea.*

A man in a green waistcoat was waiting by the farthest case. The case was empty. The man was Dowe.

"Alderman Boyle," Dowe said. "A splendid choice. The boy has exceeded himself."

"He said you required a gentleman of distinction?"

"I did. I do. Please, step inside."

Dowe opened the door of the empty case. Boyle looked at the door. He looked at Dowe. He looked at the door again.

"I don't understand."

"The exhibit requires a figure. I have the case. I have the placard. What I lack is the figure. You will stand, I will close the door, and the patrons will form their impressions. It's the work of an hour, perhaps two."

"You wish to place me inside a glass box?"

"Briefly, yes."

"As what?"

"As yourself."

Boyle had been an alderman for eleven years. He had once delivered a speech on the subject of night soil that had been reprinted in a pamphlet. He had never been asked to stand inside anything.

"This is absurd," he said.

"It is," Dowe agreed, "and yet I require it."

A placard had already been set on a brass easel beside the case. Boyle read it.

GENTLEMAN OF DISTINCTION,

PRESERVED ENTIRELY IN HIS NATURAL STATE.

Boyle read it twice. The second reading didn't improve his understanding.

"But I'm not preserved," he said.

"The placard speaks to the impression, not the method."

"And I'm certainly not keen on being gawked at."

"That remains to be seen."

Despite his reluctance, Boyle stepped into the case and Dowe shut the door behind him. Before long, the room began to fill with curious onlookers.

∞

The first patron was a woman who moved slowly from case to case, bending at the waist to read each placard aloud. She reached Boyle's case, read the placard, and straightened.

"Oh," she said.

She studied him for a long while. Boyle, uncertain of the protocol, stared at a point on the opposite wall and tried to compose his face into an expression befitting preservation. He wasn't sure what such an expression looked like. He settled on mildly thoughtful.

"The wig is very fine," the woman said at last. She said it to a companion who had not yet arrived. The companion, when she came, agreed that the wig was very fine.

"Is it real hair?" the companion asked.

"But of course," said the first woman.

They moved on to the pipe.

Boyle exhaled, which caused a brief panic in a nearby child who had not previously understood him to be breathing. The child was led away. A clerk took his place, looked at Boyle for perhaps four seconds, wrote something in a notebook, and moved on without comment. Boyle found the clerk's indifference more upsetting than the child's alarm.

Then came a student, who stood directly in front of the case and crossed his arms.

“Extraordinary,” the student said. “You can tell he’s a thinker.”

Boyle straightened slightly.

“Look at the brow,” the student went on. “The weight of it. This is a man who ponders heavy subjects.”

Boyle had never, in all his years in government, heard himself described this way. Deputies had called him thorough. His wife, on occasion, had called him a bore. No one had ever called him a ponderer.

The student produced a sketchbook and began to draw.

∞

By the second hour, Boyle had a small crowd.

They didn’t speak to him. They spoke about him, which was a different and in some ways superior arrangement. He learned that his bearing was noble, and that the cut of his coat suggested a man who had traveled but not too much. One person pronounced him "the finest specimen in the room," which Boyle didn’t think was a high bar, given the guinea pig, but he accepted the compliment anyway.

Perhaps most importantly, no one asked Boyle to sign anything. No one approached with a grievance concerning a neighbor's chimney or the placement of a new streetlight. For the first time in eleven years, Boyle's office was not in session.

He found he was enjoying himself.

A young woman wept in front of the case. She had come to see the Cromwell hair, but instead found herself transfixed by the distinguished gentleman. Boyle felt something he couldn’t immediately classify. Dignity, perhaps. Or its neighbor.

At four o'clock Dowe opened the door.

“That will do for today,” he said.

Boyle stepped out of the case, stiff at the knees. The parlor had emptied. The frog floated undisturbed.

“You did very well,” said Dowe.

“I simply stood there.”

“Precisely.”

Dowe pressed a dollar into Boyle's palm. Boyle looked at it. He hadn't expected payment. He hadn't expected anything. He had been asked to stand inside a box, and he had done so, and now there was a dollar in his hand.

"Tomorrow?" Dowe said.

Boyle opened his mouth to decline. What came out was, "At what hour?"

The Bad Boy of Beef Lake

•••

Many lake monsters have become household names:

Nessie, of Loch Ness, needs no introduction.

Champy, of Lake Champlain, has his own baseball team.

And Old Normie, of Lake Norman, was the subject of a popular miniseries.

And then there are those who, for whatever reason, have not captured the public's imagination. Chief among them is Beefy, the so-called "Bad Boy of Beef Lake."

Beefy isn't completely unknown, however. The village of Beefport has built its entire economy around him. Caps, mugs, and t-shirts all bear his likeness. It seems Beefy has been monetized in every way imaginable.

For a small fee, you can shake hands with a man wearing a Beefy costume. For a few dollars more, you can sit on his lap.

At the local diner, you can order a dish called Eggs over Beefy, although I don't recommend it. At the boardwalk, you can take a thrilling ride on the Beef-o-Whirl, which I also don't recommend.

The tourists arrive by the busload and boatful, eager to gorge themselves on these creature comforts, regardless of whether they catch a glimpse of the monster who adorns their fanny packs.

While Beefy is often portrayed as a cute and somewhat raffish figure, the historical record paints a much darker picture. One account describes his "hideous visage" with "one eye larger than the other." Another mentions a "rotten set of irregular teeth." A visiting journalist, at an apparent loss for words, wrote simply: "Beefy is inexpressibly odd and ugly."

As to his temperament, Beefy is said to possess an inner ugliness as well. Over the years, Beefy has been accused of wrecking ships, casting spells, and hurling foul insults, to name just a few of his alleged offenses. Thankfully, the residents of Beefport are a forgiving lot. Before long, Beefy had become a loveable, and profitable, member of the community.

Beefy is not without his skeptics, of course. He has been dismissed as nothing more than a large fish or a floating log. A mass delusion, some say. A marketing gimmick, most certainly.

No one knows the truth, assuming any of this is true. Beefy has never told his side of the story, leaving only a small band of cranks and weirdos to do it for him.

One such crank was Augustus Young, who plied his trade selling beach towels on the boardwalk – Beefy surfing, Beefy sunbathing, that kind of thing. Despite his humble day job, Augustus harbored loftier ambitions. He was determined to solve the mysteries of Beef Lake once and for all.

In furtherance of this goal, Augustus created a secret society called The Hermetic Order of Sea Serpents. The Order was so secret that only Augustus knew of its existence. In order to look the part, Augustus bought robes befitting a mystic. To sound the part, he adopted the title of "Grand Inspector Inquisitor," a meaningless nickname that nonetheless sounded very important.

The Order's beliefs, though rather inscrutable, can be summarized as follows: at the bottom of Beef Lake lie the ruins of Atlantis, and Beefy presides over this lost kingdom as a sort of god-king, possessing infinite knowledge of the past, present, and future.

Scientific evidence thoroughly debunks this theory, but Augustus was undeterred. Through the use of arcane mathematical formulas, Augustus had calculated that Beefy would soon reveal himself to the world.

To fulfill this prophecy, and ultimately coax Beefy out of the water, Augustus would trek to Beef Beach every Sunday to perform a ceremony. First, he would select a piece of driftwood, and use it to draw a triangle in the sand. Then, inside of the triangle, he drew a fish. Last, but certainly not least, he would say the word *Ipsissimus* three times fast. This invocation often had to be repeated, since the word *Ipsissimus* is difficult to pronounce.

Upon completing these steps, Augustus was in the proper headspace to lift the cosmic veil. What followed was typically uneventful; an hour or so of staring at the lake in silence, followed by a light lunch, also in silence.

This went on for months, until Augustus finally had a breakthrough. One Sunday, just before lunch, Augustus noticed an unusual disturbance in the water. It appeared that an object, perhaps a large fish or floating log, was approaching the shore.

What emerged from the lake was certainly not what Augustus had expected. It wasn't a scaly serpent, as such monsters are usually depicted. Nor did it resemble the cartoon renderings plastered all over Beefport. Instead, the creature looked more like a chubby seal sporting bushy sideburns.

Before Beefy could introduce himself, Augustus launched into a speech he had prepared for this very occasion.

"Beefy, the Immortal King of Atlantis, possessor of all knowledge! It is I, Augustus Young, Grand Inspector Inquisitor of the Hermetic Order of Sea Serpents. I have summoned you today..."

Beefy sighed.

"Let me stop you right there. Yes, it's me, the so-called 'Bad Boy of Beef Lake.' But please, don't call me Beefy. I hate that stupid name. And while we're at it, I don't like being called a monster either. It's just mean."

Augustus looked a little embarrassed.

"What shall I call you?"

"I like the whole 'Immortal King of Atlantis' bit, so let's go with that. But I should point out that I'm not ancient, and I'm not immortal. I actually don't know my age, or my life expectancy. And before you ask, no, Atlantis is not at the bottom of Beef Lake. It's mostly trash down there."

Augustus grew disheartened. "Do you possess all knowledge of the past, present, and future?"

"Hardly. In fact, I possess very little knowledge. I'm just a big fish-like thing that lives in a small pond-like thing, so my worldview is quite limited."

"Then why did you answer my clarion call?" Augustus asked.

"Your clarion call? You mean drawing those shapes in the sand?"

"And the chanting," Augustus added.

"Right, the chanting. No, that didn't bring me up here. You see, I generally steer clear of you cranks and weirdos, but something has been weighing on me lately and I figured you might be able to help me out."

Augustus perked up at the suggestion. "Of course, I'd be happy to!"

Beefy paused. "Tell me, Augustus, why aren't I more famous? I mean, yeah, I'm famous in Beefport, but who cares? I want a Loch Ness Monster level of fame, with the books and the movies and the spicy fan fiction! Even Old Normie got a miniseries, and he's a total bore! If you ask me, I think most of these supposed 'lake monsters' are completely made up. So what gives? Am I too ugly? Have I wrecked too many ships, cast too many spells?"

Augustus considered the questions posed. "Well, I think fame involves a certain degree of luck. It requires the right timing, the right environment, the right people."

"But maybe *now* is my time, Augustus. Maybe *this* is the place. Maybe *you* are the right person."

"I'm just a humble mystic," Augustus said. "I don't concern myself with the material world."

"Hogwash. I've seen you hawking beach towels with my face on it."

"True, but I must finance my passions somehow."

"How much money have you made off me? A lot? A little?"

"Somewhere in between."

"All without my express consent! So in exchange for your theft of my intellectual property, I think it's only fair that you pay me back."

The talk of money made Augustus squirm.

"I'm a little short on cash right now," he said. "It's the slow season."

"I'm not talking about money, Augustus. I'm talking about art! I want you to make a movie about me."

"A movie?"

"Yeah, and a good one too, not some low-budget flop. It has to be so good that not only does it make me famous, but it also makes *you* famous."

"But I've never made a movie before."

"And until recently, you weren't in a secret society either. Now look at you, the Grand Inspector Inquisitor having a chit-chat with yours truly!"

"I suppose I could try."

"Now that's the spirit, Augustus! How about you work up an outline and we'll meet back here next week to discuss?"

Augustus didn't have time to formally accept this proposal. Beefy had already disappeared back into the lake.

The encounter left Augustus swimming with ideas. He immediately returned to his beach towel kiosk and feverishly wrote the film that would propel him to stardom.

The movie would begin with a discussion of how some lake monsters are more famous than others. Examples would be given. He would then introduce Beefy, and discuss his relative fame in Beefport. For context, he'd sprinkle in a few historical anecdotes. After that, he'd talk about himself and the Hermetic

Order of Sea Serpents, including a general overview of its rituals and formulas. All of this exposition would culminate in the dramatic final scene: the first ever face-to-face interview with the reclusive Bad Boy of Beef Lake!

This could work! Augustus thought.

Augustus dutifully typed up his outline and brought it to Beef Beach the following Sunday. Once again, he selected a piece of driftwood and drew a triangle and fish in the sand.

Ipsissimus, Ipsissimus, Ipsissimus.

He stared at the lake for an hour, then ate his lunch. Beefy was nowhere to be found.

Week after week, Augustus returned to the beach, outline in hand. He drew the shapes, chanted the words, stared at the lake, and ate his lunch. Despite his timely devotion, however, Augustus couldn't repeat his one and only success. He would never see Beefy again.

"I don't need Beefy anyway," Augustus concluded. "I'll just make an unauthorized biopic. That will show him! And perhaps a new line of beach towels for marketing, and..."

Ipsissimus,
Ipsissimus,
Ipsissimus.

A Romance in Double-Entry

•••

I have always prided myself on being a man of order. Not merely organized, but orderly in the deeper sense: a man whose socks are folded in accordance with their drawer, whose meals arrive at their appointed hour, and whose opinions are arranged alphabetically for ease of retrieval. This disposition has served me well in the employ of the Borough Council, where I hold the rank of Deputy Assessor of Miscellaneous Revenue.

It was in this capacity that I was dispatched to the Oneida Community, a notorious settlement of utopians, ne'er-do-wells, and practitioners of what they called "free love." My assignment was straightforward. The Council, in its infinite and rapacious wisdom, had decreed that all amorous activity within its jurisdiction must henceforth be taxed at industrial rates, alongside foundries, mills, and breweries. I was to inform the inhabitants and commence the levy.

I arrived with a thick ledger, a sharp quill, and a most officious stamp. My instructions were clear: catalogue every sigh, every kiss, and every instance of prolonged ribaldry, then apply the appropriate tariff. My superiors had furnished me with a conversion table. A lingering glance was valued at half a farthing. Handholding fetched a shilling. Anything requiring the removal of garments was taxed at the maximum of five shillings, with a surcharge for violin accompaniment.

∞

I was greeted at the gate by a man in a billowing robe who introduced himself as Brother Ezra. He clasped my hand with such enthusiasm that I briefly considered charging him for excessive tactile demonstration.

"Welcome!" he said. "We've been expecting someone like you."

"Someone like me?"

"Someone official. Someone with a stamp."

I produced the stamp. Brother Ezra studied it carefully. He turned it over, held it to the light, and pressed it against his forearm. The purple insignia of the Borough Council displayed on his skin.

"Magnificent," he said.

I took the stamp back and stuck it in my pocket. "If I may proceed to the matter at hand," I said.

"Of course! But first, you must sample our pudding."

The pudding, it turned out, wasn't optional. Before I could read a single clause of the Council's decree, a woman called Sister Abigail emerged from a nearby orchard and thrust a spoon into my hand. She was tall, sharp-featured, and looked at me like she was measuring my worth.

"Eat," she said.

I ate. The pudding was average, at best. I recorded this observation in the margin of my ledger: *Pudding, communal, one spoonful. Unremarkable. Taxable at half a farthing.*

When I finally managed to announce the new tax, it wasn't well received. I read the decree with proper gravity, enumerating the categories of affection and their corresponding rates. I had prepared a chart, which I displayed on an easel I had carried from the Borough for this purpose.

The crowd studied the chart. Someone asked whether a sneeze counted as a sigh. Someone else inquired about the tax implications of dreaming. Brother Ezra suggested that if love were to be taxed, then taxation itself should be loved communally, and was there a rate for that?

I asked everyone to form an orderly queue and declare their affections in triplicate. They formed a circle instead. I asked them to stop holding hands. They tightened their grip.

"In Oneida, all is married to all," Brother Ezra explained. "So you may address your invoices accordingly."

I didn't know how to address an invoice to everyone. I attempted to assign each member a numerical designation, but they kept switching places. By dusk, my ledger contained nothing but a column of scratched-out numbers and a smear of pudding.

I retired to a hammock strung between two apple trees and stared at the blank pages of my book. A single firefly traced an erratic path above my face. Even the insects here refused to travel in a straight line.

∞

I would not be bullied by utopians. By the second morning, I had devised a strategy. If the Oneidans wouldn't declare their affections voluntarily, I would observe and record them myself. I would become, in effect, a field naturalist of love, documenting the mating habits of the commune as one might catalogue the behavior of exotic birds.

I stationed myself behind the woodpile with my ledger open and my quill at the ready. Within the hour, I had witnessed the following: Brother Ezra embracing Sister Constance beside the well. Two shillings. Brother Tobias reciting verse to Sister Margaret on the porch. One shilling, plus sixpence for rhyming. Sister Abigail gazing at me from across the yard with an expression I couldn't classify. Half a farthing, pending review.

By noon, the observations were mounting. By evening, they had become unmanageable. The Oneidans generated affection the way a foundry generates slag - ceaselessly, as a byproduct of their primary operations. I couldn't write fast enough. My hand cramped. My quill wore to a nub. I requested a second quill from Brother Ezra, who gave me an entire goose instead.

"We don't use the feathers for writing," he said. "We use them for tickling."

I declined to inquire further. I plucked the goose myself, fashioned a replacement quill, and resumed my work.

The Community, upon learning that their every embrace was being catalogued, didn't retreat into modesty. They escalated. They began performing their affections with deliberate extravagance, parading past the woodpile in pairs and trios, and staging elaborate serenades beneath my hammock. A barrel containing some three hundred apples was wheeled before me and declared "tokens of universal love," each to be taxed individually.

Despite my best intentions, the utopians had bested me. I went to sleep that night beneath a mountain of paperwork, holding a single, confused goose.

∞

By the third morning, I awoke on the ground. My hammock had been repossessed during the night. The goose was sitting on my chest.

I was informed that a "Romantic Tribunal" had been convened in the barn and that my attendance was compulsory. This was alarming for many reasons, primarily because I knew this tribunal lacked any legal standing.

Nevertheless, the barn was packed. Every Brother and Sister had assembled on rows of hay bales. Brother Ezra presided from behind an overturned trough. He wore his billowing robe and an expression of mock solemnity. Sister Abigail sat to his left, arms folded, looking at me in the way a cat looks at a bird.

"The Tribunal will now hear the case of the Borough Council versus Love," Brother Ezra announced. "The prosecution is represented by Deputy Assessor George Willoughby. The defense is represented by everyone else."

I objected to the format, the venue, and the defendant. My objections were overruled by acclamation.

Brother Ezra then produced my ledger, which had been lifted from my satchel during the night. He began reading my entries aloud, transforming my dry observations into bawdy theater. "Brother Tobias reciting verse to Sister Margaret, one shilling plus sixpence for rhyming," became, in Ezra's rendition, a tale of star-crossed lovers defying a tyrant's toll. My notation of "three hundred apples, tokens of universal love, taxable individually" was cited as evidence of "agricultural promiscuity." The crowd roared.

I fainted, which was immediately noted in the minutes as a "scandalous dalliance with gravity."

When I came to, Brother Ezra had reached his summation. Taxation, he argued, was the highest form of intimacy, as it bound the citizen to the state in a perpetual, obligatory embrace. If the Borough wished to tax love, then the Community would love the tax, thereby creating an infinite loop from which no revenue could ever be extracted. The logic was monstrous and, I feared, airtight.

Not to be outdone, Sister Abigail then moved that I be entered into the ledger personally - not as a tax collector, but as a taxable entity. The Tribunal agreed by a show of hands. I was now romantically entangled with every entry in my book. I found myself betrothed to pudding and scandalously involved with three hundred apples.

The stamp was applied to my forehead: ASSESSED.

I retired that evening not in a hammock but in the margins of my own ledger, surrounded by footnotes of dubious morality.

∞

The fourth day brought a discovery so unsettling that I hesitate to record it, though record it I must, for I am, above all else, a man of documentation.

My hand had begun writing words I didn't intend. I sat at the communal table with my ledger open, quill poised over a fresh page, fully intending to draft a formal complaint to the Borough

Council regarding the unconscionable conduct of the Romantic Tribunal. Instead, my quill wrote this:

George Willoughby gazed longingly at Sister Abigail, his heart fluttering like a dividend on the eve of its disbursement.

I stared at the sentence. I possessed no such flutter. I had never, in my professional or personal life, compared my heart to a dividend. The simile was not only inaccurate but fiscally inappropriate. I attempted to cross it out, but my hand wouldn't cooperate. The sentence stood firm upon the page.

I tried a different approach. If I couldn't delete the offending entry, perhaps I could reclassify it. I turned to a fresh page and attempted to file the sentiment under "Clerical Error, Non-Taxable," a category I invented on the spot for precisely this contingency. My quill refused. It wrote instead:

George Willoughby, having failed to suppress a nascent ardor, now sought to bury it in paperwork - a strategy that has never, in the history of ardor, succeeded.

The quill was editorializing. This was intolerable. An instrument of documentation has no business offering commentary on the documents it produces. I set the quill down and folded my arms, resolved to write nothing further until my hand could be trusted to obey its owner.

The quill wrote anyway. It rolled across the open page without assistance, leaving a trail of ink in its wake:

George sat with his arms folded, looking very serious and very foolish.

Sister Abigail, who had been hovering close enough to read the wet ink, leaned over my shoulder.

"I knew it," she said.

"Nonsense," I replied. "My hand has been compromised."

"Your hand writes what your mouth refuses to speak."

"My hand writes what some unseen author forces it to write. I assure you, I have no romantic designs upon your person."

"The ledger says otherwise."

She had a point. In the logic of the Community, the ledger was law. What was written was binding. I had spent three days insisting upon this very principle, and now it was being used against me with terrible efficiency.

I made one final attempt to regain control of the situation. I opened the ledger to the conversion table and pointed to the relevant line. "According to the Borough's own tariff schedule," I said, "a written expression of affection, unaccompanied by physical demonstration, is assessed at one half of one farthing. I am prepared to remit this amount and consider the matter closed."

I placed a coin on the table. It was the most dignified resolution available to me.

Sister Abigail picked up the coin, examined it, and dropped it into her apron.

"Insufficient," she said.

"The rate is clearly stated."

"But the tax is not payable in currency, Mr. Willoughby."

"In what, then?"

"Kisses, of course. And you are in arrears."

She demanded I pay my outstanding balance immediately. I opened my mouth to deliver a formal protest - I had the Latin prepared, the subsections memorized - but a strange gravity seized my arm. The author's pen, for I was now certain that some invisible narrator was controlling my movements, forced my lips forward, trembling, to deposit a single, reluctant kiss upon her cheek.

The kiss landed slightly above the jawline and lasted no more than a quarter of a second. I withdrew immediately and recorded the transaction in my ledger, hoping to establish a paper trail that might be useful in any future litigation. The entry read:

One kiss, involuntary, cheek (left), duration approx. 0.25 seconds. Rendered under duress. Not to be construed as precedent.

To my horror, Sister Abigail then demanded compound interest.

"If you kiss me once," she proclaimed, "you must kiss me again and again, until the principal is satisfied."

"At what rate?" I asked, because even in the jaws of catastrophe, a man must know the rate.

"Daily compounding," she said. "Retroactive to the date of your arrival."

I calculated rapidly. Four days at daily compounding on a principal of one kiss produced a liability of approximately sixteen kisses, assuming no grace period and a standard 360-day fiscal year. The figure was not ruinous, but the precedent was catastrophic. If the Community adopted this formula universally, the entire settlement would be engulfed in an inflationary spiral of compulsory affection from which no mouth could emerge unbruised.

Before I could present this objection, my quill scribbled furiously:

George, overcome by a sudden deficit of logic, compounded his affection at scandalous intervals.

None of it was voluntary. The narrative dragged me headlong into an embrace that was promptly audited by the Romantic Tribunal, which had reconvened in the yard for this express purpose. Brother Ezra took my stamp and applied it directly to my forehead a second time: PAID IN FULL.

Sister Abigail then insisted our romance be consolidated into a Joint Account. I swooned at the implications, but the pen merely noted:

George collapsed into her arms, thereby merging their assets.

I lay in her arms for some time, staring up at the sky. The goose wandered over and regarded us with an expression I can only describe as judgmental. I didn't record the goose's expression in the ledger. Some things are beyond the reach of documentation.

∞

It's one thing to be coerced into a kiss by a flesh-and-blood woman. It is quite another to discover that one's true passion lies with a mathematical abstraction.

On the final morning, I rose early and took my seat at the communal table before anyone else had stirred. I intended to restore some order to my ledger, which had become a disgrace to the profession. Entries were smeared, margins violated, entire pages given over to the unauthorized scrawlings of the invisible author. I needed to reassert control over my own book.

I dipped my quill and attempted to record a simple, factual observation: *Two sighs, taxable at half a farthing.* A routine entry. The sort of thing I had written a thousand times.

The ink wouldn't behave. It pooled at the nib, swelled on the page, and began to move of its own accord. The letters rearranged themselves, stretching and curving into shapes that belonged to no alphabet I recognized. The lines thickened. The figures multiplied. A column of numbers cascaded down the margin, each line producing the next in an endless, self-generating sequence.

A figure emerged from the page. Not stepping out of it exactly, but accumulating, the way a debt accumulates - gradually and then all at once. First an outline, then a density, then a presence. She assembled herself from the raw materials of my ledger: the ink, the entries, the ruled lines, the faint blue grid that had governed my professional life for twenty years.

She introduced herself as Balance Brought Forward.

She was a matronly presence, both stern and alluring, composed entirely of variables and notations. Her eyes were decimals. Her voice carried the clipped authority of a closing statement. Everything about her suggested a ledger that had been kept in perfect order for centuries and had no intention of tolerating a deficit.

I should have been horrified. I was not. For the first time since arriving in Oneida, I felt that I was in the presence of someone who understood the fundamental importance of columns.

"George," she said. "You have audited a thousand hearts, but never mine."

"I wasn't aware you had one," I replied. It was the most honest thing I had said in days.

"I don't," she said. "I have something better. I have a running total."

I understood her then. Not in the way the Oneidans understood each other - through pudding and proclamations and the indiscriminate distribution of apples - but in the way a man understands a well-organized file. She was complete. She was accurate. She didn't require a conversion table, because she was the conversion table.

I couldn't respond. My mouth was dry. My quill, however, was not. It wrote:

George, trembling, laid his hands upon her columns, tracing every entry with precision.

By now, the Community had begun to wake. They gathered around the table in ones and twos, still drowsy, rubbing their eyes. When they saw what was taking place between myself and the figure composed of ink and arithmetic, they didn't recoil. They watched with the same rapture they brought to all their ceremonies.

Balance Brought Forward and I performed our courtship in the only manner available to a man and an abstraction: through double-entry. I offered a debit of four shillings. She returned a credit of four shillings. I advanced a debit of twelve farthings. She met it with a credit of twelve farthings. Each transaction was recorded automatically, the ink flowing between us without the aid of a quill. For every figure I produced, she produced its equal and opposite. We moved in perfect equilibrium, and for the first time in my life, the books were balanced.

Brother Ezra, who had been observing from the doorway, stepped forward and placed his hand over his heart. "This," he said, "is the most beautiful thing I have ever witnessed."

"It's double-entry bookkeeping," I said.

"Exactly," he replied.

The Oneidans declared that abstractions were the purest of lovers, as they could never be taxed into exhaustion. The declaration inspired an immediate frenzy of imitation. Several Brothers and Sisters proposed entering into romantic arrangements with other mathematical concepts. Brother Ezra announced his engagement to the Pythagorean theorem, which he claimed had been courting him for years. Sister Constance declared herself betrothed to the number seven, on the grounds that it was "prime and indivisible, like my devotion." Brother Tobias attempted to elope with the concept of zero, but was talked out of it by Sister Margaret, who argued that a union with nothing could only produce nothing. Brother Tobias conceded the point, though he seemed heartbroken.

I recorded each of these arrangements in my ledger. It was the first time in days that my hand and my intentions were in agreement.

Only Sister Abigail was not delighted.

She had been standing at the edge of the crowd, arms folded, watching my communion with Balance Brought Forward the way one watches a business partner abscond with company funds. When she could bear it no longer, she flew into a jealous rage. She seized a cleaver from the kitchen and advanced upon me and Balance Brought Forward with the stated intent of separating our accounts permanently.

"I will not be replaced by a calculation!" she cried.

Her cleaver passed straight through the shimmering form of Balance Brought Forward. Abstractions are not so easily murdered. The blade met no resistance and found no purchase. It was like swinging at a column of smoke, or attempting to bisect a rumor.

But the blade pierced something. There was a sound - not a crack, but a soft tearing, like the spine of a book being broken open. Sister Abigail staggered. The cleaver fell to the floor. Her features began to blur, her outline softening at the edges. Her voice thinned to a whisper, then to a hum, then to a frequency too fine for the human ear. She was dissolving, and within moments she had been absorbed entirely into the fibers of my ledger, indexed beneath a new definition:

ABIGAIL, *n. A Sister whose affections exceed her principal.*

The Community gasped. Brother Ezra removed his hat. A petition was drafted to secure her release, but it too was absorbed by the ledger. A second petition met the same fate. A third was not attempted.

Balance Brought Forward turned to me. "Our audit is complete," she said. Then she too returned to the page - folding herself into the grid until she was indistinguishable from the entries that surrounded her. The ledger closed of its own accord.

I knew my time in Oneida had reached its natural conclusion. I packed my ledger, retrieved my stamp from Brother Ezra, and walked back through the gate. The goose followed me to the road, then stopped. We regarded each other for a moment. Then I walked on and the goose did not.

∞

I submitted my report to the Borough Council the following Monday. It was fifty pages long, heavily redacted, and concluded with the recommendation that the Community be exempted from the tax on the grounds that their romantic practices constituted an act of God, and were therefore non-deductible.

The Council denied my request. They also denied my request for reimbursement of one goose, one hammock, and three hundred apples. My appeal is still pending.

As for Sister Abigail, she remains loosely defined somewhere in the margins of my ledger. And I have returned to my desk at the Borough Council, where my socks are folded, my meals arrive on time, and my opinions are arranged alphabetically, just as they should be.

I sometimes open the ledger late at night, when the office is empty and the gaslight is low. I turn to the final page, where the ink still glistens, and I read the last entry my hand wrote of its own accord:

George Willoughby loved once, and was taxed for it. The receipt is enclosed.

How to Hold a Garage Sale

•••

Dottie St. John hadn't published a book in years. The enigmatic author, who once delighted critics and baffled readers, had faded into obscurity - her novels out of print, her awards gathering dust.

Dottie lived a quiet life in Brandy City, despite her disdain for the town and its inhabitants. Occasionally she was spotted buying groceries or returning books to the library, but mostly she stayed home, out of the public eye.

So when Dottie packed a box of unwanted things, wrote Free across the side, and left it at the curb, she thought little of it. By morning, the box was gone.

The news spread quickly - the box contained an unpublished manuscript by Dottie St. John! The press, which hadn't printed Dottie's name in years, suddenly remembered her. Once called "unreadable," she was now hailed as "the last great practitioner of the labyrinthine sentence" - whatever that meant.

Copies began to circulate, and the people of Brandy City looked upon the slim sheaf of papers with disbelief. On the title page, in stark black letters, it read:

HOW TO HOLD A GARAGE SALE

Inside, there were no labyrinthine sentences, no literary swagger. The text was simple and unassuming:

"Display merchandise."

"Price items clearly."

"Make signs."

"Offer refreshments."

This raised the question: why did Dottie St. John, the most serious novelist of her generation, write a manual for selling old lamps and teacups?

Despite the hype, initial reviews were mixed. The book was called a forgery, a joke, and a masterpiece, amongst other things.

Regardless, it wasn't long before the garage sales began. Participants carefully followed Dottie's instructions:

Display merchandise.

Price items clearly.

Make signs.

Offer refreshments.

But the people who arrived didn't buy anything. Instead, they acted very strangely.

At one sale, a man wept over a cracked vase. At another, a child refused a stuffed bear, saying: "It's not yet time."

The garage sales spread all over town, growing larger and more bizarre.

A woman placed a single shoe on her lawn and sat beside it all day. A man burned a pile of clothes and offered the ashes for a dollar. One couple sold nothing at all, but invited strangers to "browse the absence."

Inevitably, factions began to form. The atmosphere turned confrontational. Fistfights and vandalism were not uncommon.

People tried desperately to rid themselves of the book, but it only seemed to multiply. Copies thrown in the trash ended up back on the kitchen table. Copies buried in the yard were mysteriously dug up the next morning.

The town blamed Dottie, of course. They came to her house, begging for help, but she offered none.

"Page 5," she said. "No returns accepted."

Through it all, the book remained silent. Its plain sentences provided no guidance, no resolution.

As for Dottie, she had no interest in holding a garage sale of her own. She simply enjoyed watching the town tear itself apart.

Her reverie was broken by the sound of the doorbell. Dottie assumed it was another irate neighbor. Instead, she found a woman standing on the porch who bore a striking resemblance to her.

The stranger wore the same threadbare cardigan Dottie had favored for years, and her eyes held a familiar, weary cynicism.

"I'm here for the garage sale," the woman said, her voice a perfect echo of Dottie's own.

Dottie felt a sense of dread. She gripped the edge of the door, looking past the woman at her own empty lawn.

"But I'm not holding a sale," she responded, her voice trembling.

The woman didn't blink. She simply tilted her head, as if reciting a well-worn mantra.

"Page 1. Greet your customers warmly."

"I'm sorry..." Dottie began, retreating into the shadows of her foyer, but the visitor followed.

"No matter how carefully you plan, there will always be things no one wants."

The stranger leaned in close and offered a final, chilling note: "The story isn't finished until the reader is trapped inside."

The foyer dissolved into ink and vellum, unspooling Dottie's life into a knot of syntax. She was no longer the author pulling the strings, but merely another item of unwanted merchandise ready to be left at the curb.

∞

Dottie St. John was gone. Her house was left open, the rooms scrubbed clean.

The townspeople gathered at the edge of the lawn. The factions and the fistfights seemed silly now. There was nothing left to fight over.

Slowly, they entered the house. They wandered through the rooms, running their hands along the bare walls and staring into empty closets.

They stayed there for hours, and then days, browsing the absence of the woman who had finally written herself out of the story.

The sale was over, at last.

Freaks of Lightning

•••

I looked at the picture and it fell from the wall.

Let me explain.

Yesterday I was sitting at the kitchen table, and I was fiddling with a little piece of plastic that looked like a ladder. When I say it 'looked like a ladder' I mean it had vertical rails connected by horizontal rungs. You know, like a ladder. It was obviously too small to be an actual ladder. Rather, this little piece of plastic just happened to be shaped like a ladder. Its actual purpose is unknown.

I had found the ladder-shaped thing on the kitchen floor. As I mentioned, I don't know what it was. Or why it was there. The floor was otherwise spotless. I'm guessing the ladder was a component of something larger. I doubt it traveled far. Or maybe it did.

I looked around, but I didn't see anything missing a ladder piece. As I scanned the room, my gaze fell upon a painting. It's the only artwork in the kitchen, and my entire house for that matter.

I'm being generous by calling it art. A crude rendering of slippers is more accurate. It's a pastel-on-canvas mess entitled *The Magician's Slippers*.

The painting was gifted to me by a magician I once knew. The magician had chewed up a pair of my slippers, which were very dear to me. The chewed-up slippers were also a gift, given to me by another magician. That magician collected slippers and gave me a pair as a token of our friendship. Sometime later, these very slippers were chewed up by another magician, either out of boredom or spite. I'm not sure which. Either way, instead of replacing the slippers he had destroyed out of boredom and/or spite, the masticating magician gave me an ugly painting of slippers instead.

The actual slippers were ugly too, even before they were chewed on, so I suppose the painting was an accurate depiction of ugly slippers, as opposed to an 'ugly painting of slippers.' To be clear though, the painting is ugly as well. It's an ugly painting of ugly slippers. There, that settles it.

Regardless, I was staring at *The Magician's Slippers* when suddenly the painting's wood frame cracked. This was a shame, because the frame was quite attractive. More attractive than the painting, that's for sure. Nevertheless, the glass shattered next, and soon the whole ensemble came unmoored from the wall. Within seconds, the ugly painting and its once-attractive frame was reduced to a heap on the kitchen floor.

I'm certain I caused this to happen with my mind. I'm confident I could do it again. My intense staring, coupled with my fierce loathing of the painting, must have activated a form of telekinesis, hitherto dormant until now. I suppose I could, and should, develop this wild talent of mine. Surely there must be a market for this type of skill.

At this point, with all my rambling about magicians and slippers and *The Magician's Slippers*, you must think I'm mad. That's fine. But telekinesis is not unheard of. In fact, I once knew a man who destroyed his entire home simply by pointing his finger.

It was a day like any other, and he was seemingly a man like any other. Sitting at his kitchen table, much like I had been, he casually pointed at a hutch across the room. Poof! It burst into flames. He then pointed at the refrigerator, and it too went up in smoke. Every time he pointed, a new fire broke out. The dining table blazed. The bookshelf smoldered.

His powers weren't limited to fire-starting either. His finger could send objects flying across the room. Chairs fell over, got up, and fell over again. Potatoes and onions took flight. Before long, the house was a complete and utter wreck.

The man never confessed to destroying his own home, but it was pretty obvious he was the culprit. He was remanded to prison and placed in a cell with a prolific thief known as The Slipper Snatcher. The Snatcher fancied himself a magician, and introduced himself as such. "I'm a magician," he said plainly.

The Slipper Snatcher not only stole slippers, as his name suggests, but all manner of footwear. He looted loafers, shoplifted sneakers, and made off with moccasins. His thievery was always in public, and always under the nose of an unsuspecting victim. Upon noticing their predicament, the shoeless ones would slink home, embarrassed.

The Slipper Snatcher ran amok for years, amassing an enormous collection of shoes, until his luck finally ran out. He was caught red-handed with red high heels. His arrest caused a media frenzy. Ironically, an angry mob threw shoes at The Snatcher as he was escorted to jail. He loved every minute of it.

A few months into his confinement, an inmate was placed in the adjoining cell. His new neighbor had stolen the Snatcher's media spotlight by destroying his house in spectacular fashion – by pointing! – and for no particular reason.

The Slipper Snatcher tried to converse with the pointing vandal, but each time the man would fall into a trance. He simply could not, and would not, speak. Instead, when the Snatcher asked a question, an answer would appear imprinted on the vandal's arm – a dog, a horse, a ladder.

Did I mention I once knew a magician? Several, in fact. One magician appeared on my front porch. I don't know why he chose my door, of all doors. I didn't know him, nor did I care to know him, frankly. He was unkempt and uncouth. Foul breath. Very stinky.

Despite my repulsion, I have a soft spot for the downtrodden. And that is how the shabby little magician became my housemate for a time. I found him agreeable, mostly. He was quiet. He didn't mind sleeping on the floor. He never complained about eating table scraps.

Our domestic tranquility was short-lived, however. Soon the magician began suffering bouts of frenzy, which I was powerless to prevent. He tore down my curtains and bit holes in my books. The last straw came when he chewed my slippers, the pair I received from the famous Slipper Snatcher. The magician's idiotic gnawing rendered them unsightly and unwearable.

I was very upset, and decided to rid myself of the magician. I lured him into my car on the pretense of a leisurely country drive. Ten miles into this sojourn, I pulled over and ordered him out of the car. He looked very sad and confused standing there by the side of the road as I drove away.

Two weeks later, I had all but forgotten about that mangy magician. I lead a very busy and fascinating life, so I can't dwell upon every drifter who blows onto my doorstep. So there I was, leading a busy and fascinating life, when I see the magician walking toward my house. He was sniffing his way along, nose upturned, nostrils flaring. He smelled his way home!

Seeing him on the porch, I couldn't hold my grudge any longer. I flung open the door and greeted the magician warmly. Much to my surprise, he looked up and immediately bid me farewell. That was it – he left as soon as he arrived!

As a parting gift, he left me the ugly painting I described earlier. *The Magician's Slippers*, the inscription read.

I don't know if the magician painted the work himself. If so, he's a terrible artist. Perhaps he commissioned an untalented friend to paint it. Who knows? Unfortunately, I couldn't pose this question to the magician. He disappeared into a plume of green vapor.

That evening, I hammered a nail into the wall and hung *The Magician's Slippers* in my kitchen. By then I had already forgotten about the magician and his strange departure in a plume of green vapor. After all, I lead a busy and fascinating life, as you are aware.

I settled into an easy chair and stared at the painting. I admired my handiwork – the picture was level and flush against the wall. I didn't admire the painting though. Did I mention how ugly it was?

Suddenly a misty blob entered the room. At first I thought it was a cloud of gravy, as I had just watched a film about gaseous condiments. But no, this wasn't airborne gravy. It was the magician! I was sure of it.

I reached out and tried to poke the inscrutable mass. I was rewarded with an electric shock that rendered me unconscious. When I awoke, frazzled and fried, there was a horse in the room with me. The horse cheerfully said "good morning!" and then stepped on what remained of *The Magician's Slippers*, destroying that dreadful painting once and for all.

The horse neighed and disappeared in a plume of green vapor. Again with the vapor! I didn't try to touch it this time.

With the horse out of the picture, and the painting of the picture, I had a moment to look myself over. I immediately noticed images imprinted on my skin. A dog, a horse, a ladder.

I pointed at the ceiling and it caught fire. I pointed at the bookshelf and it too was set ablaze. The walls burst apart, the clapboards breaking loose. Around the house I went, until it was all destroyed.

∞

I never truly understood Feathers. Or perhaps I understood him too well, which is worse. He was one of those people who drift into your life sideways, slipping through some conversational gap you didn't realize you'd left open. One moment you're discussing the weather, and the next he's explaining how he once painted a pair of slippers so hideous they caused a roof to collapse.

Feathers wasn't a magician, though he traveled with several. He wasn't a painter, though he painted constantly. He wasn't a bird, either, though he once insisted he had survived a fall from a great height simply by 'remembering how wings worked.'

Before *The Magician's Slippers* ever hung in a kitchen, before it shattered under the force of a man's telekinetic loathing, or was trampled by a horse, it was merely a bad idea in Feathers' head. But Feathers was loyal to his bad ideas. Loyal to a fault.

According to Feathers, the painting began with a rumor about a pair of slippers stolen by a magician who lived in a cupboard. He also described a green vapor that drifted through time and space, imprinting a triad of dogs, horses, and ladders onto unsuspecting skin. Feathers said he heard all this long before it happened; rumors, he argued, travel faster than facts.

Compelled to capture the essence of these slippers before reality could sully them, he set up his easel and began to work. His technique, in his own words, was simple: "You paint them uglier than they have any right to be."

The slippers emerged slowly: first the outline, then the sag, then the unmistakable air of footwear that had suffered profound indignities. He added shadows that belonged to nothing and highlights that contradicted those shadows. A faint green haze appeared around the edges – not by design, but because, as Feathers put it, "the vapor wanted in." When he finished, the work looked exactly as it would years later: ugly, accusatory, and slightly damp.

He delivered the painting to a magician – not the slipper-chewing one, but another magician entirely, one who collected shoes surreptitiously. Feathers handed over the canvas with great ceremony, and the magician accepted it without enthusiasm.

Feathers vanished shortly afterward. He didn't vanish in a puff of smoke; he simply wandered off and didn't wander back. Nonetheless, the painting remained, traveling from house to house, offending everyone who looked at it. Feathers claimed he never intended for it to inspire such disgust, but he was the sort of man who never said the same thing twice.

Still, I believe him, or I believe the version of him that existed on the day the visions began leaking out of the future and onto his canvas. Feathers claimed he saw a man – a perfectly ordinary man – staring at a painting with such intense loathing that the frame cracked, the glass shattered, and the wall buckled. Then the man pointed at the ceiling and it caught fire. He pointed at a bookshelf and it exploded into flames. Feathers didn't know the painting was his own. Not yet.

∞

Feathers didn't intend to meet the Slipper Snatcher. No one does. The Snatcher appears only when you are distracted, vulnerable, or wearing shoes to which you are sentimentally attached. Feathers was all three, carrying his freshly wrapped painting under one arm while the visions of vapor and talking horses still buzzed in his head.

"Nice shoes," a voice said.

Feathers froze; compliments about footwear terrified him. He turned to find a man whose eyes sparkled with mischief and whose pockets bulged with stolen sandals. This was the Slipper Snatcher – not yet famous, but already on his way.

The Snatcher stepped closer. "Those are fine shoes you've got there. Very fine. Exceptionally fine."

"They're not for sale," Feathers said.

"Oh, I don't buy shoes," the Snatcher replied cheerfully. "I attract them."

Feathers took a step back. The Snatcher took a step forward. It was a dance, of sorts.

"What's that under your arm?" the Snatcher asked, eyes narrowing. "Looks like a painting."

"It's nothing," Feathers said. "Just a mistake."

The Snatcher's grin widened. "I adore mistakes. They're so collectible."

Feathers tried to walk away, but the Snatcher followed.

"May I see it?"

"No."

"May I hold it?"

"No."

"May I steal it?"

"No!"

"You've got the look," the Snatcher said. "The haunted look. The look of a man who has seen things he shouldn't have. Things involving vapor, perhaps."

Feathers stiffened. "How do you know about the vapor?"

The Snatcher shrugged. "I know many things. I know, for instance, that whatever you're carrying isn't meant for you."

Feathers clutched the painting to his chest.

"Let me help you," said the Snatcher. "I'm very good at delivering things to their rightful owners. Shoes, mostly. But I'm expanding my portfolio."

The Snatcher lunged for the painting, but Feathers shoved him aside and ran back to his studio.

∞

Shaken by the encounter, Feathers felt an uncharacteristic urge to explain himself. He sat at his desk and wrote a letter to the future owner of *The Magician's Slippers.*

Dear Future Owner, (or Current Owner, depending on when you read this, or Past Owner if you're reading this in some sort of temporal loop, which is entirely possible given the circumstances),

I am writing to warn you about the painting you now possess. Or will possess. Or should avoid possessing if you have any sense.

The Magician's Slippers are not ordinary slippers. They are not even extraordinary slippers. They are ugly yet prophetic, which is the worst kind.

I didn't intend to paint ugly, prophetic slippers – no one does – but the vapor insisted. What vapor, you ask? Never mind. It's hard to explain.

This artwork may cause certain symptoms: a faint humming, a green haze, strange and terrible visions, and the symbols of a dog, a horse, and a ladder appearing on your skin. Don't panic. They are temporary. Usually.

If the painting begins to glow, don't stare at it. If you do stare at it, don't blame me for what happens next. If you blame me, please do so in writing so I can file it appropriately.

Yours regretfully, Feathers

Feathers was proud of his letter. He placed it in the nearest mailbox immediately.

The next day, there was a knock on Feathers' door. He wasn't expecting company. He avoided company on principle.

He opened the door and found a man looking utterly bewildered.

"I'm sorry," the man said. "I think I'm here too early."

"Too early for what?"

"To buy your painting. Well, not buying it from you. From a thrift store. Later. Much later."

"You're the future owner?"

"I'm Bud Dixon," the man said. "I find *The Magician's Slippers* in a thrift store. I buy it ironically because it's so ugly. I hang it in my kitchen, also ironically. My hatred of it grows until one day it falls off the wall and ruins my life."

"You got my letter, I take it?"

"I did, but you should know I'm not the only future owner."

"Who are the others?"

The man shook his head. "I don't know. First it destroys my kitchen, then a horse steps on it, and then it vanishes in a puff of green vapor."

"A horse?"

"A very polite horse. Lovely manners."

"This is worse than I thought," Feathers said, pacing around the room.

"I should go. I'm not supposed to stay long. My kitchen is probably on fire already."

In the corner, the painting hummed.

∞

People assume the vapor began in a laboratory, or a magician's hat, or a swamp. Wrong. It began in a pantry. My pantry, to be precise, although I don't recall stocking it with vapor. I keep all sorts of notions, lotions, and potions, but not vapor. Yet one day I opened the pantry door and out came a faint puff – green, unmistakable, and entirely unwarranted.

I slammed the cabinet shut. I'm not in the habit of tolerating vapor in my pantry. I prefer my vapor outdoors, in the clouds, or in the breath of strangers. But the puff persisted. I opened the door again and the puff had grown into a plume. How many puffs constitute a plume? A lot. Believe me. Or don't.

The vapor grew larger, greener, more confident. I tried to trap it in a jar. The jar refused. I tried to sweep it with a broom. The broom snapped. I tried to ignore it. The vapor became offended.

It took over the kitchen, then the hallway, then the bedroom. I considered charging it rent. I even drafted a lease agreement. Much to my surprise, the vapor made *me* sign the lease instead. I was now the vapor's tenant, in perpetuity it seems.

The neighbors complained, as they do. They said my house smelled of vapor. I told them vapor has no smell. They disagreed. They're stupid, you see. I conceded the point anyway. It's easier to concede than to argue with stupid people. That's a rule I live by.

I tried consulting an expert. The expert consulted a book. The book consulted another book, which had been out of print for decades. Eventually, a consensus was reached: the vapor was not a gas, not a liquid, and not a solid. It was some sort of grievance. Against whom, or for what, the expert couldn't say.

One evening, the vapor spoke, in its own way. The impression of a dog, a horse, and a ladder appeared on my skin. I recognized the triad immediately. I began to suspect the vapor had been sent. By whom? Perhaps the Slipper Snatcher, seeking revenge. Or the magician I abandoned by the roadside. All plausible. None confirmed. The vapor refused to clarify. It only grew thicker, greener, more insistent.

It seeped into my dreams. I dreamt of kitchens on fire and paintings that stared back. I dreamt of a man pointing at things, and the things obeying. I dreamt of a horse who introduced himself with impeccable manners and then vanished before I could ask him anything useful. When I awoke, damp and confused, the vapor had rearranged my furniture. Whether this was an improvement is a matter of opinion. Mine was no.

∞

The magician wasn't famous. He wasn't even competent. He lived in a cupboard, which speaks volumes. He called the cupboard his stage. He called the cupboard his audience. He called the cupboard his destiny. He was an idiot.

The magician had one trick, if you can even call it that. He chewed slippers. He chewed them in public, in private, in silence, in frenzy. He chewed velvet, leather, rubber, and corduroy. He chewed until slippers were pulp. He chewed until his teeth ached. He claimed this was magic. He claimed this was art. As I said, he was an idiot.

The magician also claimed that he owned the vapor. "This vapor is mine," he declared. The vapor disagreed. It drifted away – out of the cupboard and into the world. The magician chased it all over town. He shouted, "Return to me!" The vapor ignored him, and rightfully so. It had already found better accommodations in my pantry, and later in my lungs, and later still in my dreams. The vapor was, if nothing else, upwardly mobile.

The magician wandered the streets – slipperless, vaporless, hopeless. He told strangers, "I created the green vapor." They laughed. They threw shoes at him. He caught them and chewed them. No vapor came, only indigestion. He told himself he was still a magician. He told himself he was still important. He told himself the vapor would return. None of this was true, but conviction is its own kind of magic, I suppose.

The magician eventually landed in prison. On what charges, I'm not sure. He professed his innocence, as most do. The vapor followed him to the jailhouse, an unindicted co-conspirator. It slipped through the bars and settled in.

The magician was placed in a cell next to the Slipper Snatcher. The Snatcher was delighted. He introduced himself immediately, rattling off his triumphs and tragedies, recalling every shoe he had ever stolen. He had a ranking system. Slippers were worth the most points; galoshes the least. The magician listened intently. The vapor hovered between them, noncommittal, like a guest at a party who hasn't decided which conversation to join.

The Snatcher tried to befriend the vapor. He complimented its color, its texture, its mysterious origins. The vapor refused his advances, as per usual. It imprinted symbols on his arms instead. Dog, horse, ladder. The Snatcher didn't mind. He showed the markings to the other inmates with the enthusiasm of a man showing off a new tattoo. They applauded. The magician grew jealous.

"The vapor is mine," the magician insisted through the bars. "I created it. It lived in my cupboard."

"Your cupboard," the Snatcher replied, "couldn't contain a sneeze."

"It did, I swear!"

"Keep telling yourself that."

The vapor ignored them both. It had business elsewhere.

One evening, without warning or provocation, the vapor expanded. It poured out of the magician's cell, filling the corridors with green air so thick the guards could taste it. It entered every cell, touched every inmate. Dog, horse, ladder – the triad appeared on arm after arm after arm.

Then the pointing began. An inmate aimed his finger at the wall of his cell. The wall crumbled. Another pointed at the ceiling; it sagged and collapsed. A third pointed at the floor, which was arguably a mistake, but the floor obliged and gave way regardless. Throughout the prison, fingers were raised and structures answered. Concrete cracked. Steel buckled. Bars peeled apart. The guards, who had not been imprinted and were therefore powerless, could only stand and watch as the building dismantled itself around them.

Without walls to confine them, the prisoners easily escaped into the open air, blinking at a sky they had nearly forgotten existed.

The magician climbed atop a pile of rubble and claimed victory. "This was all my trick!" he shouted, striking the pose of a man who has rehearsed this moment for years.

The Snatcher, perched on a neighboring pile, shouted louder: "I harnessed the vapor, not you!" He was already wearing a pair of shoes he had stolen from a guard during the confusion.

The vapor said nothing. It drifted away, indifferent, leaving them to argue in the rubble over who deserved credit for a catastrophe neither of them had caused.

The prison was now empty, and therefore no longer a prison.

∞

I should have known it would end this way. The vapor was never content to simply hover, imprint, and vanish. It wanted more. It wanted a home.

I returned to my kitchen, or what remained of it. The walls were gone. The bookshelf was a memory. The painting, naturally, had vanished – only the nail remained, jutting from a bare stud. I stared at the nail. I pointed at the nail. Nothing happened. Whatever wild talent I had briefly possessed had packed its bags and left with the vapor.

Speaking of the vapor: it surrounded me now, thick and proprietary. It seeped into my pores, settled in my lungs, and took up residence in the spaces between my thoughts. Before long, I found myself drifting from house to house, looking for a cupboard to call my own. People asked what happened. I told them I didn't know, which was true, and that I didn't care to know, which was also true, mostly.

∞

I was in a thrift store staring at a painting. I had gone to the store looking for a saucepan, and I walked out with a painting. This isn't unusual for me. I have a long history of entering stores with practical intentions and exiting with objects that ruin my life.

The painting cost two hundred dollars, which was the exact amount of money I possessed. I don't recall paying for the painting, but a receipt later appeared on my arm, so I suppose the transaction occurred.

On the back of the canvas was a signature: *Feathers.* Beneath it, a penciled note: *The Magician's Slippers, Version 1. Sold a better version to Phil Bitzen.*

I didn't know Phil Bitzen, but I instantly disliked him. Anyone who owns a better version of something I have is automatically my enemy. This is a rule I live by. It has caused many problems, but I stand by it.

I decided that I must find *Version* 2. I needed to understand why Feathers had created multiple versions, and why I – of all the fools in the world – had been saddled with the inferior one.

The painting grew larger. I don't mean metaphorically. I mean it physically expanded - it now reached from floor to ceiling. I touched it, which was a mistake. My finger sank into the surface.

The signature changed. It now read: *Bitzen's version is melting.*

I was pleased to learn that Bitzen's version was melting. When I pressed my ear to the canvas, I heard applause.

∞

I found myself occupying three rooms simultaneously: my kitchen, the thrift store, and a parlor covered in melted butter. I don't recommend this particular arrangement. In the kitchen, the painting was perpetually falling from the wall. In the thrift store, I was caught in a recursive loop of bumping into the same confused man. And in the parlor, I was constantly slipping on a puddle of melted butter. I tried to protest, but every time I opened my mouth, it filled with feathers.

I should clarify something before Feathers arrives, because once he does, clarification becomes impossible. People assume that when an artist makes his entrance, he does so politely – perhaps with a flourish, or a bow. This is wrong. Feathers didn't enter a room. He took over the room. He unfolded like a bad idea. He assembled himself the way a rumor does: out of fragments, contradictions, and misplaced confidence.

"Bud Dixon," said Feathers, although his mouth didn't move. "You must decide whether to be a collector, or a canvas."

Before I could answer "neither," my mouth filled with feathers again. It was annoying, to say the least.

From somewhere behind me, came a muffled voice I didn't recognize: "Return it while you still can!"

But returning things has never been my strong suit. I once tried to return a pair of ugly slippers, and look where that got me.

∞

Phil Bitzen stood in the dusty clearing behind the community center, adjusting the straps of a uniform he had ironed for the occasion. Around him, the other reenactors stretched and yawned, lazily rehearsing lines they had already memorized into oblivion.

Phil lived for this – the structure, the rhythm, the comforting weight of a past that stayed exactly where it was supposed to. He loved the polite, predictable applause. He loved the way the sequence made him feel like a small, reliable gear in a much larger machine. Gears don't improvise. Gears don't surprise anyone. Gears just turn.

What Phil did not love – and what he feared with a quiet, stomach-churning intensity – was improvisation.

Improvisation was the gateway to what he privately called 'narrative rot': a reenactment of a reenactment of a reenactment, where no one could remember which version was actually canon. Phil had never improvised a day in his life, which made what happened next feel less like a choice and more like a tectonic shift in his own biology.

It occurred during the first volley. The line of reenactors raised their muskets, barked their orders, and fell in the carefully choreographed sequence that had been perfected over decades of repetition.

Phil, scheduled to fall last, instead found his hand moving of its own volition. He lifted it above his head, just high enough to catch the late afternoon sun, and performed a gesture that had no place in the reenactment, or in any reenactment, or in any history that anyone had bothered to invent.

He flipped everyone the bird.

The battlefield froze. The muskets went silent. The audience gasped in unison. Phil stared at his own hand, horrified to find his middle finger still fully extended and trembling with a strange, defiant energy. It was the most honest thing his body had ever done, and he wanted no part of it.

"That's not in the script," someone hissed.

"It wasn't in last year's version, either," whispered another.

"It has never been in any version," said the director, appearing at Phil's side. His eyes were cold and perfectly rehearsed.

Phil tried to explain, but his voice felt thin. "I don't know what happened. My hand, it just..."

"Your hand committed heresy," the director said.

"Heresy seems like a bit much for a finger," Phil countered feebly.

"It is the only word that fits. You have introduced an unauthorized movement into a sacred loop. You have contaminated the rehearsal."

To Phil, who understood the precarious nature of things that repeat themselves, 'unauthorized movement' sounded less like a reprimand and more like a death sentence.

The other reenactors began to back away, as if the finger were a symptom of a highly contagious madness. The director pointed toward the exit.

"Leave your uniform. Leave your props. Leave the script. You may keep your shoes, but I suggest you use them to walk very far away."

Phil folded his jacket with the same obsessive care he had once given to the history he was now banned from repeating. He lingered over his script – its margins crowded with years of notes, corrections, and small drawings of forts – before leaving it in the grass. As he walked away, the reenactment clicked back into motion behind him, sealing over the gap as if he had never existed at all.

∞

When Phil arrived home, he found a small wooden crate sitting on his porch. The return label was brief and cryptic: *Feathers (Handle With or Without Care)*.

Inside, resting on a bed of damp straw, was a sculpture carved entirely from butter – a glossy, pale yellow interpretation of the dog-horse-ladder triad. The tag identified it, with unsettling certainty, as *The Magician's Slippers, Version* 2.

The detail was haunting. Phil could see the tiny ridges where Feathers' thumbs had pressed into the dairy, shaping the slippers with precision. Each crease and fold had been rendered in butterfat with the devotion of a Renaissance sculptor working in marble, if the Renaissance sculptor had lost his mind and his access to marble simultaneously. On the back of the tag, a scribbled note read:

Phil, This is the butter version. Not the better version. This typo caused Bud Dixon much consternation. My apologies. Love, Feathers. P.S. Don't eat it.

Phil stared at the note. Then at the sculpture. Then at the note again.

"Butter?" he asked aloud. The sculpture didn't respond, naturally.

He rushed the sculpture to the refrigerator, his mind already churning with questions – about Feathers' baffling artistic process, about the choice of butter as a medium, but while he was debating the logistics of returning a perishable hex, the sculpture made its own plans.

Phil looked up to find a trail of greasy footprints leading up the wall, across the ceiling, and out the front door. By the time he gave chase, the sculpture was already a block away, melting steadily in the sun as it slid toward a busy intersection. It soon rounded a corner and slipped into a thrift store.

Phil, following close behind, burst into the store and immediately slammed into a man clutching a hideous painting of slippers.

"Don't buy that painting!" Phil yelled.

"Says who?" the man asked, dazed from the collision.

"Phil Bitzen!"

The customer's expression changed. A flicker of recognition crossed his face, followed by something darker – the look of a man encountering his own enemy for the first time and finding him disappointingly ordinary. He flipped the canvas over to reveal a revised note on the back: *The Magician's Slippers, Version 1. Sold a butter version to Phil Bitzen.*

The versions had finally met. The convergence made the store feel briefly misaligned, as if the floorboards were trying to remember a different arrangement, or a different town entirely. *Version* 1 quivered in Bud Dixon's hands, while the greasy, melted remains of *Version* 2 pooled under Phil Bitzen's feet.

Phil felt that familiar, recursive tug – the same involuntary force that had hijacked his finger on the battlefield – murmuring that this collision wasn't an accident. It was just another rehearsal.

∞

Phil Bitzen had lived in Fort Lonesome his entire life, which may explain why he clung so desperately to scripts.

The origins of Fort Lonesome are appropriately murky, as befits a town named for a sentinel that never existed. While no physical evidence of a fort was ever unearthed, the locals refused to let a lack of history sully a perfectly good civic identity. They decided that if a fort hadn't stood there, it certainly ought to have, and they set out to will one into being.

The resulting structure was an unremarkable wooden cube that was quickly declared the 'authentic version' of Fort Lonesome. Once the timbers were in place, the town required a backstory. Naturally, they invented a battle. It didn't matter who the combatants were – settlers, soldiers, unruly geese – the town simply agreed the conflict had been 'decisive, historic, and certainly worth charging admission for.'

To honor this fabricated bloodbath, they began to reenact it. At first, the performances were charmingly primitive: men in ill-fitting uniforms, women in bonnets, and children wielding sticks. They shouted, they fell, they rose, and the small audience cheered. It was all rather wholesome, provided you didn't think about it too hard.

Over time, the reenactment mutated. A younger, more cynical generation began to restage the way their parents had interpreted the battle, carefully mimicking every misplaced shout and accidental stumble. This led to the 'reenactment of the reenactment,' a performance of pure gesture where soldiers saluted the shadows of soldiers and cannons fired blanks at blanks. The mythology thickened and then thinned into an unrecognizable shadow of a lie, until the town wasn't honoring a battle at all, but rather the act of pretending to have one. The distinction, once obvious, had been rehearsed out of existence.

∞

The multiplication of the forts began quietly. No one noticed the second structure at first; it was smaller, tucked behind the original, and seemed to have sprouted like a fungal growth after a heavy rain. The town historian, also a reenactor, immediately declared that Fort Lonesome had always been two forts, and that the residents had simply forgotten the second one. A common occurrence, he assured them, in a town built on selective memory.

Soon, a third appeared, then a fourth. Each subsequent fort was smaller and more intricately detailed than the last. By the time the ninth fort appeared – no larger than a birdhouse, its tiny palisades exquisitely whittled – the reenactment had grown more solemn. The actors knelt, whispered, and gestured toward the tiny structure, believing it contained the secret of the town's existence.

"Why are we pretending to fight?" someone asked.

No one answered. The question itself was immediately reenacted the following week, complete with the same inflection and the same silence.

The forts kept multiplying. They could be heard at night, creaking and splitting, birthing new versions of themselves in the dark.

∞

The forts developed an appetite for the town itself. Phil Bitzen's house was the first to be consumed. One morning, he reached for his newspaper and found his porch replaced by a stone wall; his bedroom had become a barracks, and his kitchen was now a powder magazine. His refrigerator – still faintly greasy from the butter sculpture – had been requisitioned as an armory.

The town gathered and nodded gravely: "The fort devours."

By week's end, three more homes had been absorbed. The forts began to whisper to one another, their timbers groaning commands – Advance. Hold. Fire. – in voices too earnest to ignore.

It was then theorized that the forts weren't speaking to each other at all, but directly to the residents, who obeyed without question. The mythology had finally devoured its makers. Or perhaps the makers had always wanted to be devoured, and had built the forts for precisely this purpose.

∞

The trouble deepened when the book appeared. It didn't arrive by post, nor was it discovered in a dusty attic; it was simply there one day, resting against the original fort. It was a massive, leather-bound volume, its cover cracked and weathered, its pages thick with the writing of many hands. The town immediately recognized it as *The Book of Fort Lonesome*, and within hours, it was elevated to the status of scripture. No one questioned this. Questioning things had been reenacted out of the town's repertoire long ago.

The book was not a history, however; it was an accounting of rehearsals. It contained a staggeringly precise record of every misplaced cannon, every flubbed line, and every audience sneeze from every previous cycle of the town's reenactments. It noted how, in the third year, a soldier had tripped over his own scabbard, and how, in the seventh, a woman in the front row had wept for a fictional casualty. It recorded these failures with the tenderness of a parent preserving a child's drawings – not because they were good, but because they were evidence that someone had tried.

Dutifully, the town began to reenact the book's descriptions of their own past failures. Actors played actors playing soldiers, complete with staged arguments and authentic mistakes. They found themselves caught in a hall of mirrors: were they honoring the original, nonexistent battle, or were they honoring the way they had once botched the honoring? The distinction collapsed under its own weight, and no one could be bothered to dig it out.

The book continued to write itself in real time, detailing the color of the mayor's necktie and the exact trajectory of a falling leaf. It even described the reader – standing in the square, hands trembling – realizing that their very act of reading was the next entry in the book.

∞

Then came the forgetting. It started with the architecture and moved to the mind.

First, the gate of the ninth fort vanished, followed closely by the walls of the third. The palisades blurred into a greenish haze - and here, even the most oblivious resident might have noticed the vapor's familiar tint - while the watchtower dissolved into a shadow that refused to move with the sun.

The reenactors began to lose their place, then their lines, and finally their names. *The Book of Fort Lonesome* began to shed its ink. Pages that had once been crowded with the minutiae of the town's rehearsals turned stark and white, as though the words themselves were embarrassed to be there. Eventually, the entire volume was empty, save for a single phrase that appeared on every page: *The fort forgets.*

The townspeople followed its lead. They forgot why they had built the fort, what the battle was for, or why they were standing around holding muskets. Some tried to carve their initials into the disappearing walls to anchor their identities, but the wood swallowed the carvings whole. Others wrote their names on their own arms, only to find the ink replaced by now-familiar symbols: dog, horse, ladder.

In a final, desperate act of preservation, the town established the Archive of Absence - a vast, silent hall of shelves filled with thousands of empty boxes. They spent their days meticulously cataloging what was no longer there: The Gate That Vanished. The Street That Isn't There. The Name I Used to Have. It was an accounting of the void, and they pursued it with the same devotion they had once given to the reenactment.

The more they recorded their own emptiness, the faster the remaining world retreated. Street signs faded to bare metal; gravestones shed their epitaphs until they were as smooth as river stones. In the deepest aisle of the Archive, on the highest shelf, sat a box labeled *The Truth of Fort Lonesome.* Inside, there was nothing – though if you listened closely, you could hear a faint humming.

∞

It was time for the final rehearsal. Since the town could no longer remember its past, it decided to rehearse its ending.

No one was exempt from the casting call. Families gathered in the dust to mime the ruin of their own houses, their hands tracing the outlines of walls that were already half-gone. Children lay perfectly still in the gutters, pretending to be ash. The mayor stood in the center of the square and practiced forgetting his own name, repeating it over and over until the syllables detached from their meaning and dissolved into nonsense. The reenactors applauded the performance, then reenacted the applause, then reenacted the act of remembering why they were applauding.

But the rehearsal refused to finish.

Every time the ending neared – the moment where the last light should have faded and the silence should have become permanent – someone would ruin the take. A child meant to vanish would instead sneeze and reappear. A house meant to collapse would stand stubbornly upright. A silence meant to endure would crack into a stray, nervous laugh. The director, a shadow of a man clutching a bundle of blank pages, would sigh, cross out the attempt, and declare that the rehearsal must begin again from the top.

And so it did. Over and over.

Day after day, the town rehearsed its destruction. They collapsed, burned, vanished, and fell silent, only to rise, rebuild, and remember just enough to begin the cycle again at dawn. The rehearsal had become the ending – a loop of closures that never actually closed.

The Book of Fort Lonesome added a new entry, its first in ages:

The rehearsal is the ending. The ending is the rehearsal.

By nightfall, the people of Fort Lonesome no longer knew whether they were practicing for the end or living inside it. They bowed, they fell, they vanished, and they returned, performing for an audience that – wherever they sat, whoever they were – seemed destined to applaud forever.

It was then that Phil Bitzen, who was scheduled to fall last in the ultimate sequence, found his hand betraying the script once more. He didn't fall. He didn't vanish. Instead, he lifted his hand – just above his head, just enough to catch the dying light – and flipped everyone the bird.

The book added its final entry, containing just a single word:

Lonesome.

About the Author

Ryan Kittleman's work has been called "mind-bending" (*Berkeleyside*), "darkly comic" (*Times Union*) and "kooky and delightful" (*SFGate*). He's been published in *The North American Review*, exhibited at the Crocker Art Museum, and awarded Best Animated Film at the Chelsea Film Festival, among other accolades. Originally from Upstate New York, Ryan now lives in the San Francisco Bay Area.

Also by Ryan Kittleman

Fiction

The Great Peace
The High Cost of Macaroni

Poetry

The Honorable Mentions

Film

This Is How You Cry
Edson's Gravy
Beefy!
The Following is a Paid Advertisement
How to Hold a Garage Sale

www.ingramcontent.com/pod-product-compliance
Lightning Source LLC
LaVergne TN
LVHW011338110826
845153LV00013B/456/J